Dick and Jane

READING COLLECTION • VOLUME 5

Go Away, Spot

GROSSET & DUNLAP • NEW YORK

Table of Contents

Jane and Puff

Oh, Jane.

I see something.

Look, Jane, look.

Look here.

Come, Puff.
Come here.
Jump, little Puff.
Jump, jump.

Look, Baby Sally.

Come here and look.

See Puff.

Puff can help.

Puff can help Jane.

See Puff Go

Come here, Dick.

Come and see Puff.

See Puff play.

See Puff jump.

Puff can jump and play.

Oh, Mother, Mother.

Come and look.

See Puff jump and play.

See little Puff play.

Look, Mother, look.

See Puff jump and play.

Oh, oh, oh.

See Puff jump down.

See Puff jump and go.

Jump down, funny Puff.

Jump down.

Jump down.

Go, go, go.

Tim and Sally Help

Sally said, "Look, Mother.

I can help.

See Baby Sally help.

See little Tim help.

See little Tim go.

Oh, see little Tim go."

Sally said, "Look, Tim.

Look down here.

I see cookies.

I see cookies down here.

Cookies, cookies, cookies."

Sally said. "Come, Mother.
We can go.
Look here, Mother.
Cookies, cookies, cookies.
Come, Mother, come.
We can go."

Go Away, Spot

Dick said, "Down, Spot.

I can not play.

Down, Spot, down.

Go away, little Spot.

Go away and play."

Sally said, "Oh, Spot.
We see you.
Tim and I see you.
And little Puff sees you.
We see you, funny Spot."

Dick said, "Oh, oh, oh.
Go away, Spot.
You can not help.
You can not play here."

Sally said, "Run away, Spot.
Run, run, run."

Puff, Tim, and Spot

Sally said, "See Puff go.
Puff can jump down.
Puff can run away.
See little Tim.
Tim can not jump down.
Tim can not run away."

Dick said, "Come, Spot.
You and I can play.
Look here, Spot.
Cookies, cookies.
Jump, Spot, jump."

Dick said, "See Spot.
Oh, see Spot jump."

Jane said, "Mother, Mother.
We see something funny."

"Come here.

Come here.

Come and see Spot."

Spot Helps Sally

Look, Spot, look.

Find Dick and Jane.

Go, Spot, go.

Help Sally find Dick.

Help Sally find Jane.

Go, Spot.

Go and find Dick.

Go and find Jane.

Run, Spot, run.

Run and find Dick.

Run and find Jane.